Off The Wall

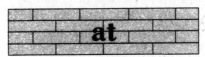

Callahan's

Books by Spider Robinson

*Denotes a Tor Book

Off The Wall

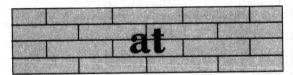

at

Callahan's

Spider Robinson

A Tom Doherty Associates Book
New York

OFF THE WALL AT CALLAHAN'S

A Tor Book
Published by Tom Doherty Associates, LLC
175 Fifth Avenue
New York, NY 10010

www.tor.com

Tor® is a registered trademark of Tom Doherty Associates, LLC.

Book design by Lynn Newmark
Interior illustrations by Phil Foglio
Edited by James Frenkel

Library of Congress Cataloging-in-Publication Data

Robinson, Spider.
        Off the wall at Callahan's / Spider Robinson.
            p. cm.
        "A Tom Doherty Associates Book."
        ISBN 0-765-31046-5
        EAN 978-0765-31046-0
        1. Bars (Drinking establishments)—Fiction. I. Title.

        PS3568.03156038 1994
        813'.54—dc20   93-43229
                                                              CIP

First Edition: March 1994

First Paperback Edition: August 2004

Printed in the United States of America

0 9 8 7 6 5 4 3 2 1

This one is for
my friend and agent
Eleanor Wood,
sine qua honest work,
with love, and thanks
for the idea . . .

and for
Captain Lazarus Long,
who established the precedent . . .

and most of all, of course,
for Jeanne,
sine qua nihil

Contents

Foreword

&

Wall Flowers

A) Begin reading here if you're not familiar with Callahan's Place [if you are, feel free to skip down to B)]:

Callahan's Place, the now-vanished tavern in Suffolk County, New York, owned and operated by Michael Callahan (a.k.a. Justin of Harmony), was an unusual establishment in many respects.

(Understatement of the millennium!)

Among the many peculiarities of that merriest of oases:

Aliens, cyborgs, transvestites, talking dogs, telekinetics, telepaths, clairvoyants, immortals, Intergalactic Traveling Salesmen, time travelers, vampires, victims of severe Tourette's syndrome, and even *editors*, were all made welcome there, from time to time.

Patrons were *encouraged* to smash their glass in the big fireplace after drinking—so long as they were willing to propose a toast first, naming the reason they felt like smashing a glass. Exercising this prerogative doubled the price of your drink . . . to a dollar. (Mike got a bulk rate on glasses.)

Punning, and competition therein, was encouraged—nay, actively abetted—by Callahan, himself a hopeless and utterly shameless paronomasiac.

Privacy was defended *by force:* any patron heard to ask snoopy questions of another patron was customarily blackjacked by Fast Eddie the piano player and dumped in the alley.

But perhaps the most remarkable and most important thing about Callahan's Place was the converse of the last paragraph: any customer who displayed any desire to discuss his or her troubles received the instant and undivided attention of not merely the bartender but everyone in the room.

Consequently, a plethora of interesting stories ended up getting told in Callahan's. All those presently known to me have

been set down in the three volumes CALLAHAN'S CROSSTIME SA-
LOON, TIME TRAVELERS STRICTLY CASH, and CALLAHAN'S SECRET
(all currently in print in Ace paperback), and collected in the
omnibus CALLAHAN AND COMPANY (Phantasia Press hardcover;
contact Alex Berman, Phantasia Press, 5536 Crispin Way,
West Bloomfield, Michigan 48033, for details).

Regrettably, the last of these stories, "The Mick of Time,"
involved the utter and final destruction of Callahan's Place, a
few minutes before midnight on New Year's Eve, 1984/5 . . .

B) Begin reading here if you already know Callahan's.

But although it is gone, gone for good, echoes of Callahan's
Place linger on.

For one thing, there is a related cycle of stories having to do
with Mike Callahan's wife, Lady Sally McGee, and the fabu-
lous bordello she once operated in Brooklyn, Lady Sally's
House—a House of *healthy* repute, and like her husband's
tavern, an equal-opportunity enjoyer. (Also, sadly, gone
now.) Two bookfuls of these stories currently exist: CALLA-
HAN'S LADY, and LADY SLINGS THE BOOZE. (I *did* warn you about
the puns . . .)

For another, a book is now available called THE CALLAHAN
TOUCH, concerning Mary's Place, the remarkable tavern
opened elsewhere in Suffolk County by Jake Stonebender
(folksinger, guitar-player, songwriter, and narrator of all the
Callahan stories) after the obliteration of Callahan's Place.

And of course, there is this book, which represents my own
desperate attempt to feed the voracious maw of ongoing Callahan Mania.

You see, another oddity of Callahan's saloon was that Mike
Callahan kept no mirror behind his bar. The wall above the
gallery of bottles—known as "The Wall," to distinguish it
from the other three—was bare and featureless . . . save for
decades of graffitti, inscribed there by Callahan himself. Any
time he heard something that struck him spoken in his bar, it

was Mike's custom to grab a Magic Marker and preserve it for posterity on The Wall. Many a newcomer found him- or herself so fascinated by this distillation of over forty years of good conversation that they ended up sitting there all night, reading and drinking and reading and drinking. (Most of Callahan's customs had more than one purpose . . . but all of them seemed to end up putting money in his pockets. Not a stupid man.)

And one day I remembered that Wall, and saw a way to get out from under a nagging problem . . .

Look: transcribing Jake Stonebender's yarns about Callahan's Place into polished and compelling prose has been putting bread on my table and music in my headphones for just short of twenty years now. *Nobody* misses The Place more than me. Ever since "The Mick of Time," the last Callahan story, was published in *Analog Science Fact/Science Fiction Magazine* in 1985, I have been reduced to thinking up stories of my own, an onerous task. Trust me: if I knew any more Callahan stories, I'd find time to set them down on paper. If I could find a way to *get* more, I would; I have tapped every source, shaken every tree, pursued every avenue.

Yet not a week has gone by—in seven years!—without at least a few plaintive letters from readers asking when I'm going to publish some more Callahan's Place stuff. People keep sidling up to me at conventions, on the streets, in public washrooms . . . imploring me to publish something else—anything else—with the word "Callahan" in the title.

I do not like to disappoint readers; they are in too good a position to redress perceived slights. So I cudgeled my brains. (I do this so often that I have had my cranium fitted with a removable screw-top, to facilitate cudgeling.) Among other things, I relived in memory—over and over again—every moment I had ever personally spent in that caravanserai of compassion. And finally one day as I was idly forward-scanning through all the mental videotape, *I happened to notice a flashbulb go off* . . .

I knew that many photographs had been taken in Callahan's Place—hell, two of my most treasured possessions are framed 8 × 10 glossies of *myself* at The Place (one jamming with Fast Eddie and Jake; the other standing at the bar with Mike Callahan's arm around me; both photos autographed by the participants). I knew at least half a dozen people likely to keep a scrapbook of such photos. In many of those pix, I reasoned, *The Wall must be visible* . . .

So I made a lot of phone calls, and I paid a lot of postage, and I made a lot of expensive trips to the East Coast . . .

. . . and then I sealed myself in my office with about a googolplex of snapshots of Callahan's Place, a magnifying glass, a Macintosh II typewriter, a stereo, a case of Old Bushmill's and two pounds of Celebes Kalossi coffee . . .

. . . and after only a million years of pain and eyestrain, I had painstakingly reconstructed something like 50 percent of the wit and wisdom recorded by Michael Callahan and imprudently stored by him on a medium inadequate to withstand a nuclear fireball. You hold it in your hands.

A large and aromatic bouquet of Wall flowers: flowers plucked from off The Wall at Callahan's Place . . .*

Yes, there was more written on The Wall than you'll find in this book—but I don't see what I can do about it unless and until more photographs surface. (If you have any, contact me c/o the publisher.)

Yes, I admit that the epigrams, maxims, perorations and pithy thayingth contained herein *do* lose something from not being scrawled in Callahan's inimitable (thank God!) hand-

---

*True story: in 1973 I had the privilege and pleasure of meeting the late great Alfred Bester. Much could be written about that meeting, for Alfie in person was the original One-Man Chinese Firedrill—but what is relevant here is that at one point he asked me what I was working on, and I said I was putting together a collection of Callahan's bar stories but couldn't think of a good title. Eyes flashing, Alfie excused himself, went to the washroom and returned less than two minutes later with a neatly typed list of over two dozen terrific titles. Among them were CALLAHAN'S CROSSTIME SALOON, TIME TRAVELERS STRICTLY CASH, CALLAHAN'S SECRET . . . and yes, by God, OFF THE WALL AT CALLAHAN'S.

I am now a firm believer in time travel . . .

Thanks yet again, Alfie, wherever you are!

writing—but not one of those photos was clear and crisp enough to reproduce well in book format.

Yes, some of these quotations, and all of the longer puns, have already appeared in variant form in diverse Callahan's or Lady Sally stories. For one thing—as in so many aspects of science fiction—there is precedent for this from Robert A. Heinlein: every word of his book THE NOTEBOOKS OF LAZARUS LONG appears in his previous novel TIME ENOUGH FOR LOVE, yet both books perennially jockey for position on Berkley Books' list of All-Time Best-Selling Titles. For another thing, in recent years people have been quoting some of these maxims and puns *to me*, unaware that I hold copyright, so it's time to set the record straight. (One reader informs me that she has been sending out Christmas cards containing the Yule Gibbons pun for years now—presumably in an effort to shorten her Christmas-card list.)

Besides, a great many of these quotes, and all the shorter atrocities, appear here for the first time.

And I have included lagniappe. Along with sayings from The Wall, I have included the lyrics to several of the songs that Jake and Fast Eddie used to play on Fireside Fillmore Nights, the ones that got the most requests during my tenure there. While only one or two of these songs actually appeared on The Wall, all of them frequently echoed *from* it, and from the other three walls. Several of these are recorded here for the first time; I've transcribed most of them from tapes in my possession, and can certify the accuracy of the lyrics.

And as if that weren't enough, I have taken special trouble to isolate the most potentially lethal quotes from off The Wall—the puns!—in separate, labeled sections of their own, for your sanitary protection.

Wisdom, laughter, and song—here you have Callahan's Place in a nutshell . . .

I know: it's not the same as having more Callahan stories. But it's *something*, and the best I can presently offer you. Half of why one went to Callahan's Place was for the companionship, the camaraderie, the merriment and melancholy, and the stories that got told, and I wish I had more of that for you, I do.

But the *other* half of why I used to go there was the consistently good conversation. Interesting things got said there a lot, because Callahan's custom of requiring a toast put his customers into the habit of distilling their (very!) varied experiences and insights into crystallized form. As the late, immortal Theodore Sturgeon used to say, "If it's really basic, it's simple." And you can't have too much of that kind of stuff.

It is my fond hope that in consideration of all this, readers will take pity on me, cut me some slack, and *not write me any more letters asking for more Callahan's Place stuff for a while.*

I promise, anything I hear, you'll hear. Okay?

—SPIDER ROBINSON
Vancouver, British Columbia
29 November 1991

C) Begin reading here if you're the kind of reader who always skips the Foreword.

Graffiti

Off The Wall
at Callahan's Place

Callahan's Law: Shared pain is lessened; shared joy is increased.

Lady Sally's Law: Shared despair is squared; shared hope is cubed (or better: Raised to the power of infinity?).

*Writing is not necessarily
something to be ashamed of.
But do it in private, and wash
your hands afterward.*
—Woodrow W. Smith

*A person should live forever, or
die trying.*
—Mike Callahan

*Most joints, the barkeep listens
to your troubles . . . but we
happen to love this one so much
that we all share his load.*
—Jake Stonebender

We raise hopes, here . . . until they're old enough to fend for themselves.

—Mike

*The church is near
But the road is icy.
The tavern is far
But I will walk carefully.*

*—Ukrainian proverb,
quoted by Charlie Daniels*

*Funny men are better lovers.
They know about pain.*

—Josie Bauer

*The average human in the best
of circumstances spends a hell
of a lot of attention and energy
on monitoring the body's
thousand and one aches and
pains and twinges and other
sudden, small alarms. At least
as much energy and time goes
into constantly combing the
environment for immediate
dangers or enemies. And as
much again is spent on worry
about impending or chronic
problems, the struggle to stay
afloat, the need to be loved, and
the underlying awareness of
mortality.
No wonder we're all so grumpy
so much of the time . . .*

—*Joe Quigley*

One man's meat is another man's person.
    —Lady Sally McGee

If you can't have fun here, it's your own damn fault.
    —Mike

There's nothing in the human heart or mind, no place no matter how twisted or secret, that can't be endured—if you have someone to share it with.
    —Jake

"*This* game's over, man! You gotta move your Boss or Rocky's gonna lay a subpoenie on him; then his Torpedo is gonna smoke your Old Lady, and all your Heavies'll be doin' time—except for maybe your Mouthpiece, but Rocky's Sheriff got him put in the corner—you got nothin' left but Punks and Junkies: you're through, Jimmy."

—Angel Martin to Jim Rockford, commenting on a chess game, in the Rockford Files episode "Chicken Little Is a Little Chicken" by Stephen J. Cannell

For a predator, a wrong guess can be preferable to a slow one.
— *Jake*

Context is everything. Breast-feeding is beneficial for nearly all infants—but for an elderly cardiac patient, it can be fatal . . .
— *Samuel Webster, M.D.*

All-purpose toast: "To all the ones who weren't as lucky."
— *Mike*

"Rupture" occurs when you think you are in the middle of a conversation with someone . . . and suddenly discover that you've merely been making noises at each other, that there is a previously unsuspected chasm between you.

—Chip Delany

Never wake up a cop by dropping a .45 on the pavement next to him.

—Joe

*If you've got a hurt and I've
got a hurt and we share them,
some crazy how-or-other, we
each end up with less than half
a hurt apiece.*

—Jake

Everybody's got roots in the past—but they's all got roots in the future, too.
                              —Fast Eddie Costigan

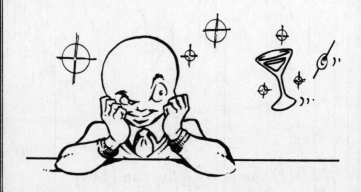

Joy always equals pain in the long run.
                              —Mike

*Joy is the product of the pain
that has gone before it,
and vice versa.*

—Rachel

*Femaleness and maleness are halves of a
spectrum, a curve on which you can graph
humanity and get a hell of a lot of overlap in
the middle. Some disparage these so-called
in-betweeners, but the true freaks are the ones
stuck way out on either end of the curve, their
sexuality unalloyed by any of its
complementary ingredient. These poor
perverts often carve wide paths through the
world, driven as they are by untempered
engines, inspiring the awe due mighty forces
out of control.*

—Maureen (last name unknown)

Suicide isn't just a cop-out; it's a rip-off.

—Jake

AUTHOR'S NOTE: *this quote was inscribed on The Wall a full decade before the debate over one's Right To Die got going. I've checked with Jake, and he confirms that the choice by a terminal patient to terminate his or her anguish does not, in his opinion, constitute "suicide."*

There is so much yammer-yammer on the air and in print these days that nobody could keep up with it, much less remember it. I mean, look at Richard Nixon's "rehabilitation." There's always somebody who didn't get the word.

—Joe

The most important step in mapmaking is to throw out all the old maps you have in the glove compartment. Forget all the reports of earlier explorers. You can't discover America if you keep shying away from the edge of the world. And if you do find it, you'll waste years asking to be taken to Kublai Khan.

—*Priscilla (last name unknown)*

Cheering someone up is a little like breast-feeding, or good sex: mutually satisfactory.

—*Jake*

Pregnant women aren't sick.
                              —Doc Webster

*We've got a world in which
physical miracles are
commonplace—and nobody's
happy. We've got what it takes
to feed all the billions of
us—and half of us are starving.
You can show a dozen guys
murdering each other on TV,
but you can't ever show two
people making love. A naked
blade is reckoned less obscene
than a naked woman. Isn't it
about time we started trying to
get a handle on love, from any
and all directions?*
                              —Jake

Get it right, you're a star. Get it half-right, you're a gas giant.

—*Joe*

"Champagne is a barometer of happiness. There is a sort of morosity everywhere."
—*Yves Bernard, chairman of Moët & Chandon, commenting on poor sales*

*Be a rapturist—the backward
of a terrorist. Commit random
acts of senseless kindness,
whenever possible.*

—Jake

*The delusion that one's sexual
pattern is the Only Right Way
To Be is probably the single
most common sexual-psychosis
syndrome of this era, and it is
virtually almost always the
victim's fault. You cannot
acquire this delusion by
observation of reality.*

—Lady Sally

A shrink's office from which laughter is not heard as often as tears ought to shut down.

—Jake

Never been to a shrink. What could be sillier than a priest who doesn't believe in the soul?

—Stephen Gaskin

Where I come from, anyone who says "Excuse me" is a human being.

—Joe

Sometimes I think I must have a Guardian Idiot. A little invisible spirit just behind my shoulder, looking out for me . . . only he's an imbecile.

—Jake

Old age is not for sissies.

—Larry Van Cott

It is usually better to not pull a gun than to screw it up.

—Mike

The only kind of payment that always guarantees a handsome return is paying attention.
—Lady Sally

It's amazing how much mature wisdom resembles being too tired.
—Commodore Aaron Sheffield

People who wear glasses are lucky; we have stars on rainy nights.
—Jake

*If you can't cut the mustard,
you can always lick the jar.*

—Mary

*Improving morale is
simultaneously one of the
noblest and most intelligently
selfish things a person can do.
Degrading morale is
simultaneously one of the
sleaziest and most stupidly
self-destructive things a person
can do.
Guess which pays better?*

—Long-Drink McGonnigle

I must have missed something: if a guy has truly absolute power, then what could you possibly corrupt him with? Acton got it backward: what engenders corruption is paranoia, the perception of inadequate power. Absolute power renders you absolutely immune to corruption.

—Mike

I like fashion—and Porsches, and Rolexes—all that stuff! How nice of the morons and drones to wear uniforms, so one can avoid them . . .

—Long-Drink

Popular myth to the contrary, drink is not really a good drug for pain. That is, it can numb physical pain, but will not blunt the edge of sorrow; it can help that latter only by making it easier for a man to curse or weep.
But alcohol is great for happiness: it can actually intensify joy.

—Jake

Hip humor: cruelty pretending to be fun.

—Mike

In our society, big lush women and small slight men go through life wrapped around a softball-sized chunk of pain; it breaks some, and makes others magnificent.

—Jake

Still I persist in wondering whether folly must always be our nemesis.

—Edgar Pangborn

Tyranny has its place. Universal freedom would deny my right to restrict Jeffrey Dahmer's recreational and dietary habits.
—Doc Webster

Over the years, I have come to learn that if you get a chance to turn anger into laughter, that will be a good thing to do.
—Jake

It claims to be fully automatic, but actually you have to push this little button here.
—Gentleman John Killian

*Long-Drink McGonnigle's Tip
for Masturbators:
Sit on your hand first, until it
goes numb.
Then it'll feel like someone else's
hand . . .*

*The only real perversions are
nymphomania, satyriasis and
celibacy . . . but even they
should be permitted for
members of a free society. The
only sex-related acts I would
proscribe—for reasons of public
health—are those involving
former food or former people,
and lying about the state of
one's venereal health or
contraceptive status.*

—Lady Sally

*Logic is a way of going wrong
with confidence.*
                    —Stinky Kettering

*A truce between the sexes? Are
you out of your goddam mind?
What else is there to distract us
all from onrushing death?
Television?*
                    —Jake

*Art takes whatever—and as
long as—it takes.*
                    —Lady Sally

Certain kinds of shit are quite palatable, with a little necessity sprinkled on them.

—Joe

What you put your attention on prospers.

—Stephen Gaskin

Sexual intercourse vests no property rights.

—Jake

Perhaps I could stand loneliness if I were not so useless; perhaps I could stand uselessness if I were not so lonely.

—Mickey Finn

"You don't even know if our species are sexually compatible."
"The hell I don't. I can see fingers and a tongue from here; anything else is gravy."
—exchange between Mickey (an alien cyborg) and Mary

Sometimes, just naming your burden helps.

—Mike

Writing is a simple trick: all you have to do is sit and stare at a blank piece of paper, until beads of blood form on your forehead . . .

—Larry Van Cott

There are places on the skull where even a gentle rap will reliably drop a man—but the back of the skull bone is not one of them. Try it yourself. Borrow a blackjack from your mother and sap a random sample of ten guys, as hard as you like. I'll bet you fifty bucks not more than four of them go down.

—Joe

So many men seem to have the idea that what women secretly want most of all (no matter what we say, or even believe ourselves) is a powerful and remorseless engine of flesh impersonally hammering away at us without pause for hours at a time. They become upset with themselves if they cannot deliver this silly commodity. I don't mean that on the one occasion in my life when it actually happened to me, it was an unpleasant experience, exactly. (Until I tried to get up and walk the next day.) It's just that maybe once in a lifetime is plenty. And I've never seen that guy since, don't much care if I do.

I mean, you could buy a machine to do that.

They exist. And women don't buy them.

Neither do gay men.

—*Maureen*

*There are two kinds of people
in the world:
those who think people can be
subdivided into as few as two
categories, and those who know
better.*
                              —Doc Webster

*From an ergonomic
engineering standpoint, the
only pardonable object in the
typical human bathroom is the
towel rack.*
                              —Mickey

I've tried my hand at matchmaking a few times, and learned that you should approach it like walking into a chemistry lab and mixing two unidentified beakers of chemicals: you might luck into a stable compound, or you might blow your hands off.

—Jake

Usually if you've got the guilts, it's because you did a disservice to someone or something you care about. So what you want to do is go and do a service for someone or something you care about.

—Jake

It doesn't have to be the same someone. It's best, but sometimes the guilt is nonspecific and it can't be. And sometimes it's too late. That doesn't matter so much. The point is just to release the pressure—equal and opposite reaction. Slow and steady, ideally. What I'm aiming for myself is to achieve balance, equilibrium, about half an hour before I die.

—*Merry Moore's codicil*

You can love only your equals or inferiors—with your superiors, compassion is the best you can do. And it's pretty damn good.

—*Mary Callahan-Finn*

*Some memories you don't want
to put words on . . . because
that would change them.
Suppose, for instance, you gave
a savage a helicopter ride. The
experience would be rich and
vivid for him. If on his return to
his village, he told friends he
had been in a little cave of ice
that flew like a bird, at first his
memories would still be true,
and different from what he
said—but the more times he told
or rethought the story, the more
"helicopter" would become
"flying ice cave" . . . which,
after all, is a lesser thing.
By naming the inexpressible,
you lose it.*
                    —Edison Ripsborn

Why *does a man try to comb*
hair over a bald spot? Is he
afraid you'll fail to notice he's
a jerk?

—Maureen

The *Nazz had them pretty*
eyes. He wanted everybody to
see out His eyes so they could
see how pretty it was.
—*Dick Buckley, speaking of Jesus*
of Nazareth

*Vengeance is
counterproductive.
Not to mention the fact that it
gets your soul all sticky.*
                    —*Lady Sally*

When I say that she played with me, for the first time in my life I mean that the way a little kid would mean it. She played with me, like a kid might play with another kid who had been whacked on the head recently and needed some diversion. Well, if this was a sane culture, I mean, and kids were allowed to have sex with each other as part of playing, like God intended.

—*Joe*

Art with contempt in it is always sour.

—*Lady Sally*

If it's sloppy, eat it over
the sink.

—*Tommy Robbins*

Now *I remember where I know
you from. I looked up "ugly" in
the dictionary and they had a
picture of you.*
—*Long-Drink to Doc Webster*

*So isn't it a pity, when we
common people chatter
of those mysteries to which I
have referred,
that we use for such a delicate
and complicated matter
such a very short and ordinary
word.*
                    —*Anonymous*

*We were not making love, we
were fucking. Nothing wrong
with that; just not enough right
with it.*
                    —*Maureen*

I've been in hospitals. They take away your pants. Then they hurt you and starve you and expose you to disease. Then they bill you. A lot.

—Joe

All humans—without exception—want to love. No organic or emotional or psychological damage can remove that need. Humans can survive, albeit in pain, without being loved—but lock a man in a dungeon and he will find an ant to love, or try to. The sociopath, who feels no emotions, wishes he could love, and is driven mad by his impotence.

—Mickey

*If you are feebleminded enough
to want to believe in good and
bad joss, the Constitution so
entitles you—but have the
decency not to try and spread
the virus.*

—Lady Sally

"*Why do men want to leave right afterward so often? When they could be cuddling and being held?*"

"*Sometimes because the intensity of the relief, the depth of their gratitude, makes them feel small or out of control. Sometimes because in their secret miseducated hearts they believe they've done something disgusting to you, and are glad of it, and so are ashamed. And sometimes just because they were doing something when the dread compulsion came over them, and now they want to get back to whatever it was.*"

—exchange between Mary and Phillip (last name unknown)

Skills are the flowers you get if you water your talent bush enough.

—Arethusa

I don't know why it should be worse to die without time for pain or regrets . . . but to me, it is. I'm not looking forward to dying—but I've spent a lifetime getting ready for it, and I don't want it stolen from me.

—Joe

"Remember what I told you, kid: life is a shitstorm—and when it's raining shit, the best umbrella you can buy is art."
—Pedro Carmichael to Martin Looder, in the film *Tune In Tomorrow, written by William Boyd*

*Try to live your life as though
one distant day, your descendants
will develop time-travel and
cloning skills, and come back to
resurrect everyone that ever lived
who wasn't a jerk or a creep.
Maybe at the end, when your whole
life passes before your eyes, it's
a high-speed data dump.
Endeavor to see that it makes you
seem worth the trouble of
reviving. Try to be the kind of
guest they'll want at
The Last Great, Never-Ending
Party At The End Of Time.
It could happen, right?
Do you know of a better shot
at immortality?*

—Sam Meade

God gave women buttocks because sooner or later they have to walk away from us, and at least this way there's some consolation.

—Joe

*Don't belittle yourself. If it
truly needs doing, let someone
else do it. There'll be no
shortage of volunteers.*
—Lady Sally

*What shall it profit a man if he
gaineth the whole world, yet he
hath no allowable deductions?*
—Mike

*Any man is willing to believe
that he was the best you've ever
had. He knew it all the time.*
—Maureen

*One can dismiss out of hand
any so-called religion that puts
out death threats on satirists. It
is self-evident that God enjoys
rough humor.*
—Gentleman John Killian

*Death to anyone wearing a
turbine.*
—*racist graffito spotted in Surrey,
British Columbia, by Mickey
Finn . . . the only person on Earth
who fits the description*

It's damned odd: the fight-or-flight adrenal rush is supposed to be the evolutionary heritage of millions of years of success in surviving crises . . . and just about every time it's ever happened to me, it ruined my judgment or my coordination or both.

—*Jake*

In a world like this, a freak is no bad thing to be. They proved that back in the Sixties.

—*Arethusa*

*There are few things on earth
as dangerous as a liberal
vigilante.*

—*Joe*

Darling, all men think about rape, at least once in their lives. Women have an inexhaustible supply of something we've got to have, more precious to us than heroin . . . and most of you rank the business as pleasant enough, but significantly less important than food, shopping or talking about feelings. Or you go to great lengths to seem like you do—because that's your correct biological strategy. But some of you charge all the market will bear, in one coin or another, and all of you award the prize, when you do, for what seem to us like arbitrary and baffling reasons. Our single most urgent need—and the best we can hope for—is to get lucky. We're all descended from two million years of rapists, every race and tribe of us, and we wouldn't be human if we didn't sometimes fantasize about just knocking you down and taking it. The truly astonishing thing is how seldom we do. I can only speculate that most of us must love you a lot.

—Mike to Lady Sally

It's hard to strike a balance between keeping an open mind and being a sucker. But you have to try . . .

—*Joe*

Religions only look different if you get 'em from a retailer. If you go to a wholesaler, you'll find they all get it from the same distributor.

—**Stephen Gaskin**

If you're raped, don't charge the bastard with rape. Charge him with indecent exposure. It is much easier to get a conviction for that charge than for rape. The defense is not allowed to ask anything about your sexual history or how you were dressed at the time. Forensic evidence is unnecessary. The total public embarrassment to you is cut more than in half. What's the guy going to do, leap up in court and say, "It's a filthy lie, Your Honor. I raped that bitch!"? In many states, a man convicted of indecent exposure will actually draw more prison time than a rapist. And weenie-waggers do harder time than anybody but a short-eyes—in fact, the scheme sort of incorporates the Law of Talion.

An eye for an eye . . .

—Mary

Anger is fear with an attitude.
—Mike

A fantasy is not even a wish,
much less an act. There is no
such thing as a culpable or
shameful fantasy.
—Lady Sally

I like my flattery plausible.
—Arethusa

Everything in your body is connected to everything else. If you doubt it, have ear surgery, and then wiggle your big toe.

—Doc Webster

Memories are the only real treasures a man has.

—Joe

"Straighten me, Nazz . . . 'cause I'm ready."
—Father Newman quoting Dick Buckley's famous rap about the Nazz(arene)

Every time I hear someone put the word "mere" in front of the word "semantics," I bite my tongue hard and remind myself that I too am greatly ignorant.

—Phillip

There aren't many things a man can do as noble as passing up a chance to show how smart he is.

—Joe

Do not waste your fear on the mighty. Cowards make the deadliest opponents—and pacifists never fight fair: they can't—and the worst thing about terrorists is how weak they are: so weak that they have to be monstrous to accomplish anything.

—Lady Sally

The distance between one and a hundred is nothing compared to the distance between zero and one.

—Joe

There's nothing wrong with wanting wars to stop—but the moment a pacifist uses any weapon but calm speech, he's a hypocrite. If he's willing to kill, he's a psychotic.

—Lady Sally

"*Thunder is good, thunder is
impressive, but it's lightning
that does the work.*"
—*Mark Twain to Nikola Tesla*

*The best nonprescription
analgesic is laughter.
Maybe analgesic is the wrong
word. If you laugh hard when
you're post-op, you hurt like
hell. You just don't give a
damn. Hard to understand how
a painful experience can leave
you feeling better, but there
it is.
Sharing the laughter makes it
even better . . .*

—Josie

You can learn as much about
someone from watching them
belly-laugh as you can from
making love with them.

—Joe

Wrinkles are your combat ribbons. Wear them proudly!
—Shorty Steinitz

A writer's real occupational hazard is carpal tunnel vision.
—Jake

When something scares you shitless, you can go back up inside your head and hide. But when the thing that scares you comes from inside your head, you . . . well, you go to a place that isn't a place, erasing your footsteps behind you. And somebody's got to come in after you . . .
—Paul MacDonald

Short of accident or hypnosis,
self-abuse is logically
impossible.
            —*Doc Webster*

The thing to do with a silly
remark is to fail to hear it.
            —*Zebadiah J. Carter*

Some delusions are necessary.
Or do you know of a rational
reason for living?
(You say you do? I won't argue:
your delusion is necessary.)
                            —Jake

*Pessimism may be a realistic
way of looking at life . . . but
who can live with that much
realism?*

—Jake

*The human race has few (if
any) problems that couldn't be
solved by massive wealth. And
we're literally surrounded by it,
like a fly in amber. Now if we
only had brains . . .*

—Ben Bova

*The worst misunderstandings
are the unspoken ones.*
—*Slippery Joe Maser*

The expression "lowest common denominator," when spoken outside the context of mathematics, is usually being misused. If used to connote contempt for something popular, it is certainly being misused. The speaker is both ignorant and elitist. The phrase does not imply that the commonest denominator is always the lowest.

—*Dr. Jacob Burroughs*

Sneering at something is an admission of failure. You are claiming superior talent or insight . . . but declining to use it. The best way to sneer at something, if you must, is to improve it or outdo it.

—Shorty

*E*rections are certainly useful
in pleasing a woman, but I've
never understood why so many
people seem to think they're
essential. Sure, they're
flattering—but a man who
doesn't *have an erection and
still wants to make love to me,
now that's* flattering.

—*Arethusa*

"Na mai kharundi, kai chi
khal tut,"
or, translated from the
Romany,
"Do not scratch where it does
not itch."
—Gypsy proverb

To approach telepathy, you start with empathy and crank that up as high as you can.

—Jake

Never carry a grapefruit.

—Lazarus Long

Why do we build refrigerators that spill money on the floor? And ovens that spill money on the ceiling? And sit them side by side, a heat-maker and a heat-loser, unconnected?

—Jim/Paul MacDonald

*The customer need not always
come first. Enjoy yourself: it's
contagious.*
*—standard advice of Lady Sally
to apprentice artists at her brothel*

*I'd rather have a bottle in front
of me than a frontal lobotomy.*
—Tom Waits

*A classic vicious circle: you
don't love yourself enough,
so you treat yourself so badly
that it's hard for you to love
yourself . . .
Be good to yourself. Maybe the
idea will catch on . . .
—Les Glueham and Merry Moore
("The Cheerful Charlies")*

Triads have a very short shelf life—unless all three members are ambisexual. For a heterosexual species with two sexes, odd numbers are unstable. If a commodity is scarce, competition for it will ensue.

Triads are as interesting as hell—while they last. But so is a chimney fire . . .

—Lady Sally

Kindness beats honesty, every time.

But think it through—and make sure you're being honest with yourself . . .

—Mike

*You got it, buddy: the large
print giveth, and the small print
taketh away . . .*
                            —*Tom Waits*

"Man alone cannot know himself. The container cannot contain itself."
"I do not understand what you mean. Do not all containers contain themselves? If not, what does contain them?"
—*exchange between Long-Drink and Mickey*

Antiabortionists fail to carry their philosophy to its logical culmination: Stamp Out Menstruation! End the Slaughter of Millions! (And try to ensure that the ratio of females to males runs several trillion to one, so that every sperm can fulfill God's Plan for it as well.)
—*Mike*

Have you ever wondered how those missionaries communicated the idea of the so-called missionary position to the Indians? How did they come to have the vocabulary? It had to be show and tell, right? "Now, never do this . . . or this . . . and especially not this . . ."

—Jake

Among the most common
thoughts that ever passed
through a human brain:
"That doesn't apply to me."
"It's not fair."
"Not again."
"I wasn't ready."
"I might have known."
"Make it not have happened."
"This can't be happening."
"I have a right." (Or, "I know
my rights.")
Note that they are all incorrect
or semantically null.
                    —Doc Webster

God damn it, you didn't write it on a "word processor"! Or even on a "computer." What it is, is a goddam typewriter—a machine for turning fingerstrokes on a keyboard into ink symbols on a piece of paper. (Okay, yours can also be used as a computer when you're not writing—my old Royal manual can be used as a nutcracker, or a paperweight, or a murder weapon.) The silicon revolution did not change that process—from the user's point of view—much more than did the electric typewriter, it merely streamlined the error-correction process. When it's being used to make words appear on a page, it's a typewriter.

To speak of your "word processor" is like referring to your car as an "exothermically powered, myocontrolled matter transporter." The only purpose of the term is to cue your listeners that you can afford to use a computer as a typewriter, and all it really tells them is that you're insecure enough to worry that people might think you still use one of those old-fashioned things to type on.

—Mike

*And "electronic typewriter" is
silly in the other direction: what
it means is a computer so stupid
that all you can do with it
is type . . .*
                              —Susan Maser

*Love is an active verb. It's not
an abstraction or a conceptual idea. You have
to perform an action to show that it's really
real.
Enlightenment is not so much making it to
Never-Never Land through the secret
passageway. It's more like getting off your tail
and doing something . . .*

—Stephen Gaskin

*Concerning whores: anyone who thinks it
immoral or exploitive or dishonest to "pay a
person to pretend to care about you" has
obviously never flown first-class . . . or gone to
a psychiatrist, or a hairdresser, or eaten in a
restaurant . . . or talked to a bartender they
don't know.*

—Mike

Politically correct euphemisms are for the differently-brained.

—Tanya Latimer

Librarians are the secret masters of the world. They control information. Don't ever piss one off.

—Jake

*Glad; sad; mad. What else
is there?*

                    —*Long-Drink*

*Think of some miraculous
thing. Any wonderful object,
okay? The moment there are
two of them, one is second-rate.
Once there are three, one is
mediocre and one is the worst.
Comparison sometimes kills
wonder . . .*

                    —*Jake*

Prostitutes function rather like priests for people who feel more comfortable confessing their sins while naked.
                    —*Father Newman*

One of the silliest preoccupations of man is the notion that it makes some kind of sense to divide whole categories of people up into one winner and a whole bunch of losers or also-rans. What poor sick compulsive first infected us all with that virus? And how?

—*Doc Webster*

"If I let them live rent-free in my head, they'll tear it up."
—black man on CBS Nightwatch, on his reaction to black women who bitterly criticize him for having married a white woman

You can't eat half a piece of shit.

—Mike

I think that there is only one church, and your membership button in it is your belly button.

—Stephen Gaskin

*It sounds so simple, but it's so
hard to do:
To laugh when the joke's on you . . .*
—tag line for an uncompleted song
by Jake

*People who hang up on your
answering machine without
leaving any message—not even
an apology for wasting your
attention—are the most
cowardly of pickpockets.*
—Long-Drink

Fellow movie fans, I'm very sorry, but there is nothing you can do with a normal car to make it blow up. At most, you might start it burning. Falling off a cliff won't make a car blow up. Only a dissatisfied business rival or a stunt coordinator can do that. Pity the hundreds of spinal cases every year who were pulled from non-burning wrecks by movie fans afraid of the "inevitable" explosion.

—Noah Gonzalez,
bomb-disposal technician

*The pessimist sees only the
darkness of the tunnel.
The optimist sees only the tiny
point of light in the distance.
The realist knows that light is
probably an oncoming train . . .*
—Long-Drink

*You are the people.
You are this season's people—
There are no other people this
season.
If you blow it, it's blown.*
—Stephen Gaskin

Meyer's Law: In any emotional dilemma, the thing you should do is the one that's hardest.
—John D. MacDonald

Looked at a certain way, people are essentially wish-generators, with no "off" switch, and they're dangerous when armed. We can't help brimming with wishes . . . and most of them would kill us or worse if they ever came true.

—Mike

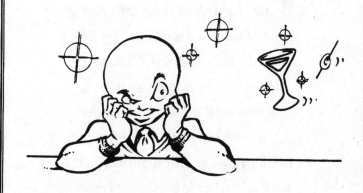

Ask the next question. Keep on asking questions and don't stop, and sooner or later you'll be asking intelligent ones. If you live long enough.

—Theodore Sturgeon

When I think of how different, how bleak and desolate my life could have been if I hadn't happened to pay attention, a decade and a half ago, to the drunken ramblings of a broken-down fellow folksinger named Jake, lab-quality freon drips into my veins.

—Spider Robinson, from the Foreword, CALLAHAN AND COMPANY

In some ways, it's nice that memory is so plastic and transient. You play differently when you know there's tape rolling.

—Jake

Please consider yourself, now and henceforth, and no matter what anyone else ever asks of you, free to do any damned thing you want that doesn't hurt someone else unnecessarily.
                    —Lady Sally McGee

Puns (I)

Set Pieces from
Punday Nights . . .

WARNING: the following pages contain material that may be deemed objectionable by more sensitive readers. Reader discretion is advised. Responsibility for any and all physical or psychological damage resulting from continued reading is hereby specifically repudiated. PROCEED AT YOUR OWN RISK; do not read further while driving, riding in any conveyance, or operating heavy machinery. "Here be stynkers . . ."

One day a planet is discovered out
Antares way whose sole inhabitant is
an enormous humanoid, three miles
high and made of granite. At first it is
mistaken for an immense statue left by
some vanished race of giants, for it
squats motionless on a yellow plain,
exhibiting no outward sign of life. It
has legs, but it never rises to walk on
them. It has a mouth, but never eats or
speaks. It has what appears to be a
perfectly functional brain, the size of a
condominium, but the organ lies
dormant, electrochemical activity at a
standstill. Yet it lives.
This puzzles the hell out of the
scientists, who try everything they can
think of to get some sign of life from
the behemoth—in vain. It just squats,
motionless and seemingly thoughtless,
until one day a xenobiologist,
frustrated beyond endurance,
screams, "How could evolution give
legs, mouth and brain to a creature
that doesn't *use* them?"
It happens that he's the first one to ask
a direct question in the thing's

presence. It rises with a thunderous
rumble to its full height, scattering the
clouds, thinks for a second, booms,
"IT COULDN'T," and squats
down again.
"Migod," exclaims the xenobiologist,
"of course! *It only stands to reason!*"
—Long-Drink McGonnigle

Did you boys ever hear of the planet
where the inhabitants were mobile
flowers? Remarkably similar to
Earthly blossoms, but they had feet
and human intelligence. The whole
planet was ruled by a king called
Richard the Artichoke-Heart, and one
day at a court orgy his eye was caught
by Fuchsia, a pale-eyed perennial. Her
beauty was so great that it *almost*
made up for her stupidity.
Refusing to believe the ancient
principle that beauty times brains

equals a constant, the smitten
monarch engaged royal tutors of all
sorts for Fuchsia, to no avail. All
failed to capture the attention of the
witless concubine, whose only
apparent interest was in gathering
pollen. At last the embarrassed
Richard gave up and had Rotenone
slipped into her soup.
As he exclaimed to his prime minister
later that night, "I can lead a
horticulture, but I can't make her
think."

—Doc Webster

(According to Jake Stonebender,
Fuchsia had a child before she
died—and dark rumor suggests that
Richard, a notoriously
forward-thinking ruler, spent his
declining years riding the Waif of the
Fuchsia.)

One night the conversation turned to Richard Adams's book SHARDIK, *about an ancient empire ruled by an enormous, semimythical bear. This triggered Doc Webster:*

The only way to become a knight in Shardik's empire was to apply for a personal interview with the bear. This had its drawbacks. If he liked your audition, you were knighted on the spot—but if you failed, Lord Shardik was quite likely to club your head off your shoulders with one mighty paw. Even so, there were many applicants—for the peasantry were poor, and if a candidate failed for knighthood, his family received, by way of booby-prize, a valuable sheepdog from the Royal Kennels. This consoled them, for truly it is written:
"For the mourning after a terrible knight, nothing beats the dog of the bear that hit you."

If you're under 35, and not passionately interested in health food, this one may go over your head. If so, count your blessings.

Until very recently, a tribe of killer monkeys lived undetected beneath Greenwich Village.

To some extent it was not surprising that they escaped notice for so long. They had extremely odd sleeping habits, hibernating for 364 days out of every year (365 in leap years) and emerging from the caverns of the Village sewers only on Christmas Day. Even so, one might have thought they could hardly help but cause talk, since they tended when awake to be enormous, ferocious, carnivorous, and *extremely* hungry. Yet in Greenwich Village, of all places on Earth, they went unnoticed until last year, when they were finally destroyed. Everyone *knows* that Yule Gibbons ate only nuts and fruits . . .

—Ralph Von Wau Wau

I commanded a submarine in Her
Majesty's Navy during the last World
War, and had at least one secret
mission. The famous spy Harry Lime,
the celebrated Third Man, had
developed a sudden and severe case of
astigmatism—and many of his
espionage activities forbade
dependence on spectacles. At that time
only one visionary in the world was
working on the development of a
practical contact lens: a specialist at Sir
Walter Reed Hospital in America. I was
ordered to convey Lime there in utmost
secrecy, then fetch him home again.
Lime was an excellent actor, of course,
but I began to suspect that there was
nothing at all wrong with his vision. I
learned that he had an old girlfriend
who lived twenty miles from the
hospital. So I called him into
my cabin.
"I can't prove a thing against you," I
said, "but I'm ordering you to go
directly from the sub, Lime, to the
Reed oculist."
—Gentleman John Killian

The toilet tanks on commercial airliners often leak. This results in the formation of deposits of blue ice on the fuselage. The ice is composed of feces, urine, and blue-liquid disinfectant. Now, occasionally, when a plane must descend very rapidly from a great height, as in the Rockies, chunks of blue ice ranging up to two hundred pounds can—and *do*—break off and shell the countryside. I have seen a UPI wirephoto of an apartment in Denver that was demolished by a fifty-pound chunk of blue ice. (The airline bought the occupants a house. Neither was hurt . . . and for a while—until it began to melt—they were actually grateful for the coolness the bolus provided. It was summer, you see, and the impact had destroyed their electric fan . . .)
So even if you live where there are no strategic military targets, you can still be attacked by an icy B.M. . . .

—Al Phee

Puns (II)

Spontaneous Conversational Eructations, Mercifully Brief

NOTE: as these are mostly unattributed, blame cannot, at this late date, be positively assessed. But it is safe to assume that better than half of them were perpetrated by Doc Webster.

We were going to explore the Kama
Sutra . . . but at the last moment, her
Kama turned into a period . . .

Be he never so humble, there's no
police like Holmes.
                                    —Bill White

The success of a pun is in the *oy* of the
beholder.

Got a date with the doctor who did my
vasectomy. She believes in reaping
what she sews.

The Buddhist hamburger joint: they'll make you one with everything.

The hackers' burger joint: you can have chips with it.

The junkies' hot-dog stand: they'll sell you one with the works.

I *know* you'd like to screw like a
bunny—but I just washed my thing,
and I can't do a hare with it.

Bulimia is one of those subjects that
can *only* be discussed ad nauseam.

He acquitted himself well at the trial.
Regrettably, the jury did not follow his
example . . .

(He was blamed for something he
didn't do. He didn't wear gloves . . .)

He learned about sex by trial and
error. Now they've got him on trial for
one or two of those errors . . .
—Ronny Corbett

Name a cowboy hero you can't even call by his first name without going insane.

ANSWER: Paladin, from HAVE GUN, WILL TRAVEL. His first name is "Wire"—it says so right there on his card: "Wire Paladin, San Francisco."—so to call him by name, you have to go, "Hey, Wire!"

The shortest distance between two puns is a straightline.
                              —David Gerrold

Songs

From the repertoire of Jake
Stonebender and Fast Eddie
Costigan, as performed on
Fireside Fillmore Nights
at Callahan's Place—

Those unattributed must be
assumed to have been written
by Jake and Eddie.

❧ The Drunkard's Song ❧

A swell and wealthy relative of mine had up and died
And I got a hundred thousand from the will
So a friend and I decided to convert this into liquid
*   form*
The better our esophagi to fill
So we started in the city, had a drink in every shitty
Little ginmill, which is really quite a few
Then a cabbie up in Harlem took us clean across the
*   river*
Into Brooklyn, where he joined us in a brew
We was weavin' just a trifle as we pulled into Astoria
At eighty miles an hour, in reverse
But it was nothin' to the weavin' that we did as we was
*   leavin'*
And from time to time it got a little worse
*   Well, there's nothing like drinkin' up a windfall*
*   We was drunker than a monkey with a skinful*
*   So goddam drunk it was sinful—and I think I ain't*
*   sober yet*

We was feelin' mighty fine as we crossed the city line
Suckin' whiskey and a-whistlin' at the girls
But the next saloon we try, a fella wants to black my
*   eye*
'Cause he doesn't like my shaggy hippie curls
So then a fist come out of orbit, knocked me clear
*   across the floor*
But I was fairly drunk and didn't really care
And I was sorta disappointed when the coppers hit the
*   joint*
As I was makin' my rebuttal, with a chair

*Ah, but the coppers come a cropper, 'cause I made it to
    the crapper*
And departed by a ventilator shaft
*Met my buddies in the alley as they slipped out through
    the galley*
*And we ran and ran and laughed and laughed and
    laughed*
  Well, there's nothing like drinkin' up a windfall
  We was drunker than a monkey with a skinful
  *So goddam drunk it was sinful—and I think I ain't
    sober yet*

Halfway out of Levittown, we got our second wind
In a dump so down and out I had to laugh
So I had another mug, and my friend another jug
And the hack another pitcher and a half
*When we got to Suffolk County, we were goin' into
    overdrive*
The word had spread, and crowds began to form
*We drank our way from Jericho along 110 to Merrick
    Road*
A-boozin' and a-singin' up a storm
*I lost my buddy and the cabbie in the middle of the
    Hamptons*
We was drunker than it's possible to be
*But there finally came a time I didn't have another
    dime*
I sat on Montauk Point and wept into the sea
  Well, there's nothing like drinkin' up a windfall
  We was drunker than a monkey with a skinful
  *So goddam drunk it was sinful—and I think I ain't
    sober yet*

♣ Afterglow ♣
(Iris's Song)
by
Teodor Vysotsky

Tending to tension by conscious intent,
declining declension, disdaining dissent;
into the dementia dimension we're sent:
we are our content, and we are content.

Incandescent invention and blessed event,
tumescent distention, tumultuous descent:
our bone of convention again being spent,
I am your contents, and I am content

to be living . . . to be trying . . . to be crying . . . to be
*   dying . . . (I want)*
to be giving . . . to be making . . . to be breaking . . . to
*   be taking*
all you have . . .

Assuming Ascension, Assumption, assent,
all of our nonsense is finally non-sent—
with honorable mention for whatever we meant . . .
You are my content, and I am content.

🐾 Time-Travel Blues 🐾

*You've heard of every kind of blues there is, I hear you
    say?*
*Well, I'm leavin' here tomorrow . . . and I just got back
    today*
I got the time-travel blues, look at the mess I'm in
*I'm sad for what the past will be . . . and what the
    future hasn't been.*

I longed to know the future, like the Oracle of Delphi
*And then this cat knocked on my door: Goddam, it was
    myself! I*
got the time-travel blues, since I met myself comin' in;
*I'd tell you all about it . . . but where the hell do I
    begin?*

He said that I was going to invent a time machine—
That is to say, I told me, if you follow what I mean.
I said, "I'm no inventor, man: I'll never ever get it."
*But he said, "Copy this one, and we both can share the
    credit!"*

*I cranked it up, it blew right up, and then and there I
    died.*
*I wonder who that joker was, and why the bastard
    lied . . .*
*Got the time-travel blues: one of my life's most awful
    shocks*
Now I could use a doctor: in fact, I need a paradox

If I am dead, my murderer can't logically exist
But here I am in pieces, and I'm really gettin' pissed
I got the time-travel blues—it's only natural, bein' dead
To want to think that time is really only in your head

♣ Spice ♣

And when I've just assuaged your lust
By flicker-light of telly
I love to lie between your thighs
My cheek upon your belly
To smell you and to feel you
And to hear your small intestine
And know that this is perfect bliss
Just as it was predestined

In the hour that my death draws near
And I wonder what my life was for
It'll be the afterglows
With your fragrance in my nose
I'll remember and relive once more

And now I rest, caress your breast
And sail in satiation
On the oceanic motion
Of your rhythmic respiration
And now my lips and fingertips
Are flavored sweet and sour
For I have nipped and fully sipped
My favorite furry flower

In the hour that my death draws near
And I wonder what my life was for
It'll be the afterglows
With your fragrance in my nose
I'll remember and relive once more

I know in time I'll have to climb
Up next to you for sleep
With no regret, but not just yet
This moment let me keep
And suddenly it comes to me
—how glorious and dumb!—
I had so much fun making love
I plain forgot to come . . .

♣ Please, Dr. Frankenstein ♣

I've walked a thousand miles in an effort to retain ya
And I didn't come for charity: I fully plan on payin ya
But I've been so depressive, guess I'm ready for some
mania
That's why I've traveled all this way to gloomy
Transylvania, singin:
Please, Dr. Frankenstein, won't you try and bring me
back to life?
Cause I truly have been grievin since I got "Goodbye,
I'm leavin" from my wife
I'm slowly goin nuts because the memory of her cuts me
like a knife
Please, Dr. Frankenstein, won't you try and bring me
back to life?

I cannot seem to find my pulse; my temperature is
down
And I can tell I smell like hell, the way that people
frown
I feel like rigor mortis, all I do is lay around
You gotta help me, Frankenstein, I'm halfway in the
ground (I'm beggin)
Please, Dr. Frankenstein, I am up for any kind of
change
Spent evenings in this coffin just a little bit too often,
and it's strange
Please don't consider me more than some flesh for you
and Igor to arrange
Please, Dr. Frankenstein, I am up for any kind of
change

I'll stagger like the victim of a wreck
I'll wear those funny bolt-things in my neck
I'd love to be in stitches—what the heck
Do you need cash, or will you take a check?

I'm not afraid of what you'll do—I'm immunized to
  pain
Cause everything I ever had has bubbled down the
  drain
Make me the Pride of Frankenstein and I will not
  complain
Just strap me down and let me have a transplant of the
  brain: I need it
Please, Dr. Frankenstein, won't you try and raise me
  from the dead?
My heart is barely beatin since I caught the woman
  cheatin in our bed.
My entire world's a coffin and it doesn't get me off, an
  like I said
Please, Dr. Frankenstein, won't you try and raise me
  from the dead?

❧ Come to My Bedside ❧
by
Zaccur Bishop

Come to my bedside and let there be sharing
Uncounterfeitable sign of your caring
Take off the clothes of your body and mind
Bring me your nakedness; help me in mine . . .

Help me believe that I'm worthy of trust
Bring me a love that includes honest lust
Warmth is for fire; fire is for burning
Love is for bringing an ending to yearning . . .

For I love you in a hundred ways, and not for this
   alone
But your lovin' is the sweetest lovin' I have ever known

Come to my bedside and let there be giving
Licking and laughing and loving and living
Sing me a song that has never been sung
Dance at the end of my fingers and tongue

Take me inside you and bring up your knees
Wrap me up tight in your thighs and then squeeze
Or if you feel like it, you get on top
Love me however you please, but please . . . don't stop

For I love you in a hundred ways, and not for this
   alone
But your lovin' is the sweetest lovin' I have ever known

I know just what you're thinking of:
There's more to love than making love
There's much more to the flower than the bloom
But every time we meet in bed
I find myself inside your head
Even as I'm entering your womb

So come to my bedside and let there be loving
Twisting and moaning and thrusting and shoving
I will be gentle; you know that I can
For you I'll endeavor to be quite a singular man . . .

Here's my identity, stamped on my genes
Take this my offering: know what it means
Let us become what we started to be
On that long-ago night when you first came with me . . .

O, lady! I love you in a hundred ways, and not for this
    alone
But your lovin' is the sweetest lovin' I have ever known

🐾 Out of Your Way 🐾

You went out of your way to make sure I'd love you
And now you say be patient for a while
You went out of your way to be just as nice as you could
*   be*
Until I fell, and then you modified your style
You say you're somebody else's slave . . . I suppose we
*   all got our crosses*
But I ain't nobody's slave and I figure it's time I cut my
*   losses*
You could end up mine some way, but baby, until that
*   day*
I'm goin' out of your way by a country mile

You went out of your way to make sure that I'd need
*   you*
You taught me the significance of need
And I went out of my way to show you who I am and
*   how I fell*
Which is for me a thing remarkable indeed
You got a lotta laughs inside, but I'm afraid that's
*   where they're keepin'*
You got a lotta tears there too, and I reckon you're
*   much more fond of weepin'*
You could end up mine, it's so—but baby, until I know
I'm goin' out of your way with all due speed

You went out of your way to make sure that I'd want
*   you*
With your eyes as much as with your knowing hands
But you'll never be happy at all until you want to

And till I don't want to be makin' long-term plans
They've already dealt the hand: I'll either win it or else
     I won't
You understand how I feel and you either want me or
     else you don't
Take as long as you need to decide—but baby, I got my
     pride
And I'm goin' out of your way while I still can

—oh, can't you see?

You ain't no use to me like this: there ain't enough of
     you left to miss
Why don't you come out of your way, just one more
     time, with me?

🍂 Hardon You 🍂

I know my constant horniness gets hardon you
Sometimes it seems I'm always in the mood
If that is so, I truly beg your pardon, too
It wasn't my intention to be rude
  My love is like my horniness, in that it never quits,
  But I'd love you if you didn't have those tits

Men have only got the one thing on their mind
It gets so repetitious it's a crime
Somebody said a hard man is good to find
As long as you don't find him every goddam time
  You are not only something that I lust for, that I hunt
  I would love you if you didn't have a cunt

I'm neurotically erotic, with a taste for the exotic
And your body is hypnotic when it's next to me
I'm dementedly attentive, and in need of no incentive
But you know you represent much more than sex to
  me . . .

You know that I was horny for you from the start
And that's the way it's always gonna be
But you ought to know your sexiness is just a part
Of the value you will always have for me
  It may have been what caught my eye: it isn't why I
    stick
  I would love you if I didn't have a dick.

🐾 Mountain Lady 🐾
(Jeanne's Song)
by
Spider Robinson

*Mountain Lady, sing for me: your singing makes me
glad to be alive
Mountain Lady, give to me your lovin', for it helps me
to survive
Mountain Lady, stay with me, and let me drink your
beauty with my eyes
I want you to lay with me, and be there in the morning
when I rise*

*You give me what I need, and you need what I can give
Like you, I live for loving, and like me, you love to live
I swear I'll make you happy if there's any way I can
And if you will be my Mountain Lady, I will be your
man . . .*

*Mountain Lady, smile for me: your smile is like the
rising of the sun
Wait a little while for me—I'm coming back as fast as I
can run
Mountain Lady, talk with me, for talking is essential to
our growth
I want you to walk with me through all the days
remaining to us both*

*You give me what I need, and you need what I can give
Like you, I live for loving, and like me, you love to live
I swear I'll make you happy if there's any way I can
And if you will be my Mountain Lady, I will be your
man . . .*

Mountain Lady, dance for me,
Your dancing takes my breath away, you know . . .
Save that loving glance for me—I love it when you let
*   your loving show*
Mountain Lady, give to me a kind of love I've never had
*   before*
I want you to live with me: I cannot live without you
*   anymore . . .*

You give me what I need, and you need what I can give
Like you, I live for loving, and like me, you love to live
My love is deep and stronger than a river running wild
I want to be your lover, and the father of your child . . .

Dramatis Personae

I believe in my heart of hearts—and in my brain of brains, for that matter—that an epigram should be like a good son-in-law: completely self-supporting. If it needs footnotes, it's not an epigram. My old friend and esteemed editor Jim Frenkel, however (like clams, he's better esteemed than eschewed), is certain you will find the epigrams in this book more enjoyable if you know a little something about their speakers. And he is quite keen that you enjoy yourself, since he has overpaid me so outrageously for this volume and wants to be sure you'll give copies to all your friends for Christmas. Who could argue with that? Well . . . me, for one.

My feeling is that if you finish this book curious to know more about the people whose wit and wisdom hold its covers apart, the sensible thing for *me* to do would be to just refer you to the six available volumes in which they appear at much greater length, and hope you take the bait.

But in all fairness, I have to admit that might not be the most sensible thing for *Jim* to do, as none of those six books is published by this house just now. (Although Jim was the editor who bought the first Callahan book . . . and was working for Tom Doherty at the time! Life is strange.) [Editor's note: At presstime, this has been corrected. Tor has just bought the first three Callahan books and the next Mary's Place book, CALLAHAN'S LEGACY.] Therefore I bow to his editorial insight, marketing savvy and phenomenal endurance in argument.

Here, then, are as few words as I can get away with concerning all the wonderful people you've heard quoted. (The descriptions in italics are quoted, and sometimes misquoted, from Chris McCubbin's excellent text for the CALLAHAN'S CROSSTIME SALOON role-playing game, available from Steve Jackson Games, Inc., of Austin, Texas.)

MIKE CALLAHAN: *He built his bar in Suffolk County, in the image of countless other roadside Irish taverns in the New York area . . . a serene and reassuring presence, he always kept his place merry. He looked like a big dumb Irishman, but it was impossible to talk to Callahan for more than a few minutes without realizing that he was a man of unusual depth, wisdom and sensitivity . . . from Big Beef McCaffrey, who tried to shortchange him, to the Mafia flunky who tried to scare him into renting a jukebox, anybody who tried to put the muscle on Callahan got the same treatment—a free trip to the parking lot, and probably a broken bone to remember it by. He smoked big cheap cigars that he lit with non-safety matches. His reverence for human dignity, privacy and liberty verged on the religious. He never mentioned his subjective age. It is assumed that he's about the same age as his wife, who is well into her third century.* Mike was born centuries from now, in a place (possibly a planet) called Harmony. Since it has taken me several books to even outline his mission in this ficton (a technical term for a space-time locus), I won't attempt it here. CALLAHAN'S SECRET has the best summary, I think. Suffice it to say, he is a good guy.

LADY SALLY McGEE: *Lady Sally was Callahan's spouse and counterpart in a battle across time. She opened her famous brothel, Lady Sally's House, in Brooklyn at the height of WWII, when such enterprises were tolerated . . . By the time the war was over, she had so many influential friends that there was no question of closing her place down. A tiny, trim redhead who spoke in a patently phony British accent, Lady Sally was not an incredible beauty. It was not her features, but her manner that accounted for her astonishing sexual appeal. She considered sex an art, and studied it extensively. Her employees were called "artists" (not "prostitutes," and never "whores" or "hookers"). Her artists were paid a regular salary plus room and board and allowed to keep any (optional) tips. Her clients paid according to their means. Her artists were of all seven sexes, and she catered to all sexual preferences except the dangerously violent. Her Ladyship is much tougher than she looks, and has fewer scruples than her husband about killing evil people.*

MARY CALLAHAN (now Mary Callahan-Finn): *The only (known) child of Mike Callahan and Lady Sally, Mary was born and raised on Harmony. When she reached adulthood, she began working for her mother, and despite what some would call a weight problem, soon established a reputation as one of the most professional and popular artists at Lady Sally's House. After a few years, she transferred to working literally behind the scenes, as her mother's chief of security. Where she got her training as a blacksmith is unknown. She is a cheerful woman with a tremendous capacity for fun and no tolerance for evasions or self-delusions.* I do *not* think Mary has a weight problem (I think very few women have a weight problem—although a lot of them have a big jerk problem), and neither does Jake Stonebender. She had a (very) brief affair with him once, but is now married to:

MICKEY FINN: *Alien cyborg, 6'11½", 600 lbs; apparent age, 40 . . .* Finn is the only survivor of a race exterminated centuries ago and far away by star-traveling monsters. They filled him with enslaving machinery and made him a scout. The very first Callahan story, "The Guy with the Eyes" (reprinted in CALLAHAN'S CROSSTIME SALOON), concerns the night he walked into Mike's Place and announced that his job required him to sterilize Earth, and he felt just *terrible* about it. The response of Callahan's patrons was to sympathize: they got him drunk. Which, happily, shorted out the machinery that made him a slave. He spent the next decade or so learning how to be human (he spent some years as a farmer), but has since left Earth with his new bride, Mary.

JAKE STONEBENDER: narrator of the Callahan's Place and Mary's Place stories. (And my financial arrangement with him is our business, okay?) *A likable, lanky man with shoulder-length hair and a beard. If he doesn't watch himself, he can get a bit strident about his liberal politics. A gifted folksinger, he loves his guitar Lady Macbeth like family. While Jake doesn't have the most brilliant mind at Callahan's, he may*

*well have the quickest. He certainly saved everyone there,
and likely the whole planet as well, through his quick actions
on the Night of the Cockroach . . . Jake used to have a wife
and daughter, until he decided he could fix his own brakes.
After their death, he tried suicide twice, and was fortunate
enough to have his stomach pumped the second time by:*

DOC WEBSTER: who prescribed for Jake a trip to Callahan's
Place, and not incidentally spared me a life of honest work. *In
many ways Sam "Doc" Webster is the leader of the gang, even
more than Callahan himself. While Mike is the unmoving cen-
ter around which the bar orbits, Doc Webster is usually the
one out there pushing the other patrons to do things, have fun
and keep The Place merry. An immense man, he is Callahan's
most profound drinker. He's also an excellent physician, who
once removed Shorty Steinitz's appendix on Callahan's bar-
top. What most people remember about the Doc, though, is his
immense, almost mythic, joyousness. He could break up the
Sphinx with a one-liner that was old when it was built. He is
the all-time Punday Night champion.*

LONG-DRINK MCGONNIGLE: *The toughest and least charis-
matic of Callahan's regulars, Long-Drink (he's "one long
drink of water," 6'7") is an indolent and independent man
with a razor-sharp tongue and no time for nonsense—unless
it's amusing nonsense. In spite of his attitude problem, Long-
Drink isn't as shallow as he likes to pretend. He genuinely
cares about people who are hurting—and not just his friends,
either. He cried openly when Jake broke Lady Macbeth.* I
would have to say that Long-Drink's sense of humor is the
most primitive in the group. And I'm going to get him back
some day . . .

FAST EDDIE COSTIGAN: *Callahan's bouncer and piano player.
Born in Brooklyn, he met Callahan after the war, at Lady
Sally's, and accepted the piano chair in the bar Mike was just
building out on Long Island. He resembles a badly shaven*

chimpanzee. As a bouncer, his technique is subtle and effective. He knows he's not as clever as the other guys at the bar, and he's comfortable with that. Still, he often surprises his friends with an unexpected insight or brings down the house with a quietly hilarious pun or wisecrack. It was he who found a way to make the broken Lady Macbeth well again. Eddie is the best damn piano man I ever hoid . . . uh, heard.

LES GLUEHAM & MERRY MOORE (a.k.a. The Cheerful Charlies): *In the early '70s, Les Moore and Merry Glueham were not happy people. As if their names weren't bad enough, they were also each out of work. With nothing to lose, each called a guy named Flannery who cheered people up for a living—satisfaction guaranteed or your money back. It worked. Tom Flannery not only cheered Les and Merry up, but when he introduced them, they fell in love. Then he gave them jobs as his assistants. When they got married, Les and Merry swapped last names—it seemed to work better that way. Tom died a few months later, as he'd been expecting to, and Les and Merry kept the business going. Their business card reads,* "HAVE FUN—WILL TRAVEL."

NOAH GONZALEZ, SHORTY STEINITZ, SLIPPERY JOE, SUSIE AND SUZIE MASER: regular patrons of Callahan's Place. Noah used to work on the county bomb squad; Shorty is the worst driver alive; the Masers have been a triune marriage ever since Joe's wives found out about each other. (It seems to serve him right.)

JIM/PAUL MACDONALD: telepathic half-brothers with a fused identity, who appear first in CALLAHAN'S CROSSTIME SALOON, and last in CALLAHAN'S SECRET. They sacrificed themselves to save the world from a cockroach.

ARETHUSA QUIGLEY: surviving incarnation of a pair of telepathic *twins*. In contrast to the MacDonald brothers, these identical blonde sisters, raised by religious fanatics who denied the concept of twinhood, grew up with only a single public identity, which they took turns investing. The story of how they moved into a single skull together is told in LADY SLINGS THE BOOZE.

JOE QUIGLEY: former private dick from New York; now gone public. He's married to Arethusa, and they worked together at Lady Sally's House in its final year. I've always thought he's a dead ringer for Dan Rather, myself, but he says he can't see it.

JOSIE BAUER: one of Callahan's best-loved regulars. A humor groupie, her unvarying custom was to offer to sleep with whoever won the Punday Night competition. Few winners, male or female, ever turned her down, or reported regret afterward. Further deponent sayeth not.

RACHEL (last name unknown): 232 years old at the time she entered cryogenic suspension in 1973. Fast Eddie visits her every week. See CALLAHAN'S CROSSTIME SALOON for details.

MAUREEN: this is probably Maureen Hooker, former artist in the employ of Lady Sally McGee, currently free-lancing as a team with her husband Willard, a legendary confidence man now retired from the game. They fell in love in CALLAHAN'S LADY.

PRISCILLA (last name unknown): Lady Sally's bouncer; sort of a female version of the Terminator—the friendly one, from the second film. Her heroic death is recounted in LADY SLINGS THE BOOZE; briefly, she died because she was bulletproof.

PHILLIP (last name unknown) and TIM (last name unknown): alumni of Lady Sally's House; see CL and LSTB for details.

FATHER NEWMAN: a Catholic priest who hung out . . . uh . . . religiously at Lady Sally's House. An organized and determined conspiracy of patrons, who attempted to nail down once and for all whether or not he ever actually availed himself of an artist's services while there, disbanded with the question unresolved. I know, but I won't tell you.

WOODROW W. SMITH, COMMODORE AARON SHEFFIELD, AND LAZARUS LONG: Yep. That guy. Very merry gent. For an explanation of how a fictional character could walk into a bar in real life, see THE NUMBER OF THE BEAST by Robert A. Heinlein.

STINKY KETTERING: all anyone remembers about this guy is that he probably came in with Lazarus Long.

ZEBADIAH J. CARTER, DR. JACOB BURROUGHS: see above note regarding W. W. Smith. It was believed at the time that these customers might be gay (despite the fact that their female companions were knockouts), since they were overheard using that word an inordinate number of times. The Heinlein novel cited above later explained the matter.

TOMMY ROBBINS: all I know is, the only surviving photo of him bears a remarkable resemblance to the guy who autographed my copy of EVEN COWGIRLS GET THE BLUES. Could be . . .

GENTLEMAN JOHN KILLIAN: his photo resembles the guy who autographed my copy of STAND ON ZANZIBAR.

LARRY VAN COTT: strongly resembles the guy who autographed my copy of RINGWORLD, down to the detail that he apparently never drank anything but Irish coffee at Callahan's. The fact that said author writes a competing series of bar stories might account for the pseudonym . . .

CHIP DELANY: looks very much like the guy who autographed my copy of BABEL-17.

EDGAR PANGBORN: If this is indeed the Pangborn who wrote DAVY and "Angel's Egg," I could kick myself for missing him at Callahan's. He's not with us anymore, more's the pity. Look him up in the library!

JOHN D. MACDONALD: again, if this was the author of the Travis McGee series and so many other fine books, I wish I'd bumped into him at Mike's place; among other things, I always wanted to ask him what Meyer's other name is, just to see how he'd answer . . .

TED STURGEON: no question, this is *that* Ted Sturgeon, one of the two best science fiction writers who ever lived. I brought him to Callahan's myself. He was Punday Night champion for eight weeks running, a record exceeded only by Doc Webster himself—and gave seminars in Unlimited Inquiry (the symbol you'll find with his quote on page 110 was part of his autograph and stood for "Ask the *Next* Question . . ."), Marriages Involving *Odd* Numbers of Spouses, and Advanced Hugging. God bless you, Theodore, wherever you are.

ROBERT A. HEINLEIN: Ted's only peer. If you don't know who he is, you should be reading one of his books instead of this one.

DICK BUCKLEY: internal evidence—and mutual friend (and folk music legend) Ed McCurdy—suggests this may have been the late Lord Buckley (the Gasser! 1907–1960), the legendary American monologist who composed and declaimed free-verse tributes to his heroes in Hipster, a dialect created by black jazz musicians and later adopted and adapted by white jazz musicians, beatniks, hippies and other undesirables. C. P. Lee states that, like Louis Armstrong, His Lordship never performed without firing up a large pipe of marijuana first; unlike Pops, he did so onstage. Lee also claims that Buckley and an entourage once crashed a Sinatra concert at the Waikiki Sheraton, stark naked. (George Harrison's song "Crackerbox Palace" was named for Lord Buckley's home.) Though his frame be long stashed, His Lordship's surviving records are well worth the trouble of seeking out.

TOM WAITS: yes, this would seem to be the well-known pop star, songwriter, actor and former jazz singer—who once gave me permission to quote his song "$29 and an Alligator Purse" in my novel MINDKILLER, in exchange for $29.00. (Guess he didn't need a purse . . .)

STEPHEN GASKIN: a preacher and semiretired wizard, who taught classes on spirituality at the Family Dog back at the dawn of the Hippie Era, crossed the continent with a convoy of school buses, and eventually founded the most successful of the hippie communes, The Farm, in Summertown, Tennessee. (It's still there—and so is he—but the last time I visited, they were pointedly ignoring each other.) At its peak, The Farm consisted of 1,000+ freaks on 1,000+ acres, totally self-supporting and living in harmony with their rural neighbors. Their international disaster-relief arm, Plenty, was praised as a model by the Canadian government. Nowadays The Farm is a corporation: you own shares, or some such; and I'm not sure what happened to Plenty, since everyone I knew in it has quit.

I got no use for gurus and holy men. Irish whiskey works just fine for me. But I'm willing to punch the ticket of Stephen, and of one of *his* teachers, Shunryu Suzuki-roshi—because neither of them ever claimed to be any more than a guy who'd had a few minutes to think, and had noticed some interesting things.

One quick Stephen story that may make my point: he gets up from dinner one night in the early '70s to answer the door. There stands an awestruck young man who says he's just walked here from the Coast because he's decided his mission in life is to follow Stephen around and record his every utterance for posterity, unobtrusively and at the lad's own expense. Stephen gently closes the door in his face and returns to the table. "Who was that?" asks his wife, Ina May. "A temptation from the Evil One," Stephen murmurs, and finishes his soyburger . . .

That's my kind of preacher. Which is partly why I wrote the introduction to his latest book, HAIGHT-ASHBURY FLASHBACKS (Ronin Press, 1992). To give you an idea, its original 1980 edition was titled AMAZING DOPE TALES.

CHARLIE DANIELS: one of my oldest and best friends in the world; directly responsible for my move to Canada in the '70s; presently straightening spines and otherwise practicing chiro in Yarmouth, Nova Scotia. The Lucky Duck, who appears in the current book THE CALLAHAN TOUCH, bears a bit of a resemblance to Charlie. Less sarcastic, though . . .

ANONYMOUS: a Callahan's regular, so self-effacing that no one can recall much about him. Not even how he got that name, which I'm sure we must have asked. In fact, I'm not sure he isn't still around Mary's Place somewhere (the bar Jake opened up after Callahan's Place was destroyed).

SAM MEADE: a passing folksinger who ended up in Nova Scotia.

EDISON RIPSBORN: nothing is known about this customer. Related to Pangborn somehow?

BEN BOVA: yes, *the* Ben Bova, multiple-award-winning writer, ex-editor (of *Analog* and *Omni*) and space enthusiast, and my oldest friend in this business. (Well, I knew Jim Frenkel first, but neither of us was in the business then.) He became a regular at Callahan's shortly after I sold him the very first of Jake's stories about it, in 1972 . . . and he and Barbara are still seen in Mary's Place today. But not often enough . . .

About the Author

Since he began writing professionally in 1972, Spider Robinson has won three Hugos, a Nebula, the John W. Campbell Award for Best New Writer, the E. E. ("Doc") Smith Memorial Award (Skylark), the Pat Terry Memorial Award for Humorous Science Fiction, and Locus Awards for Best Novella and Best Critic. His book CALLAHAN'S CROSSTIME SALOON was named a Best Book for Young Adults by the American Library Association. His short work has appeared in magazines around the planet, from *Analog* to *Xhurnal Izobretatel i Rationalizator* (*Inventor & Innovator Journal*, Moscow), and his books are available in eight languages. Twelve of his seventeen books are still in print in the U.S. and Canada.

He was born in the Bronx in 1948, on three successive days (they had to handle him in sections), and holds a Bachelor's degree in English.

He has been married for eighteen years to Jeanne Robinson, a modern-dance choreographer, former dancer, and teacher of both dance and the Alexander Technique; she was the founder of Nova Scotia's Nova Dance Theatre, and its Artistic Director during its eight-year history. The Robinsons collaborated on the Hugo-, Nebula- and Locus-winning 1976 classic STARDANCE (Baen Books), which created the concept of zero-gravity dance, and on its 1991 sequel, STARSEED. (Jeanne was on NASA's waiting list for a Space Shuttle seat, to try out zero-gee dance in practice—until the *Challenger* tragedy ended the Civilian In Space program.)

The Robinsons currently live in Vancouver, British Columbia.